P9-DDM-194

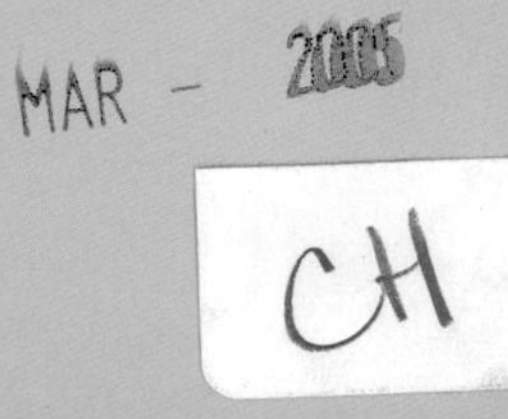
CH

Four Friends
IN
Autumn

For Barbara and Don Elleman,
who will be having autumn in
New England from now on

SIMON & SCHUSTER BOOKS FOR YOUNG READERS
An imprint of Simon & Schuster Children's Publishing Division
1230 Avenue of the Americas, New York, New York 10020

Book design by Lucy Ruth Cummins
The text for this book is set in Celestia Antiqua.
Manufactured in China
2 4 6 8 10 9 7 5 3 1
Library of Congress Cataloging-in-Publication Data
dePaola, Tomie.
Four friends in autumn / written and illustrated by Tomie dePaola.— 1st ed.
p. cm.
Summary: Four friends, Missy Cat, Mistress Pig, Master Dog, and
Mister Frog, enjoy an autumn dinner party together.
ISBN 0-689-85980-5 (hardcover)
[1. Parties—Fiction. 2. Autumn—Fiction. 3. Friendship—Fiction. 4. Animals—Fiction.] I. Title.
PZ7.D439 Fle 2004
[E]—dc21
2002013323

Four Friends in Autumn was previously published in different form, as the chapter entitled "Autumn" in
Four Stories for Four Seasons, copyright © 1977 by Tomie dePaola

Four Friends
IN
Autumn

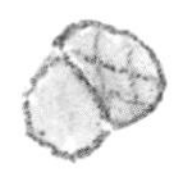

STORY AND PICTURES BY
TOMIE DEPAOLA

SIMON & SCHUSTER BOOKS FOR YOUNG READERS
New York London Toronto Sydney

One crisp fall day Mistress Pig invited her three friends to a dinner party.

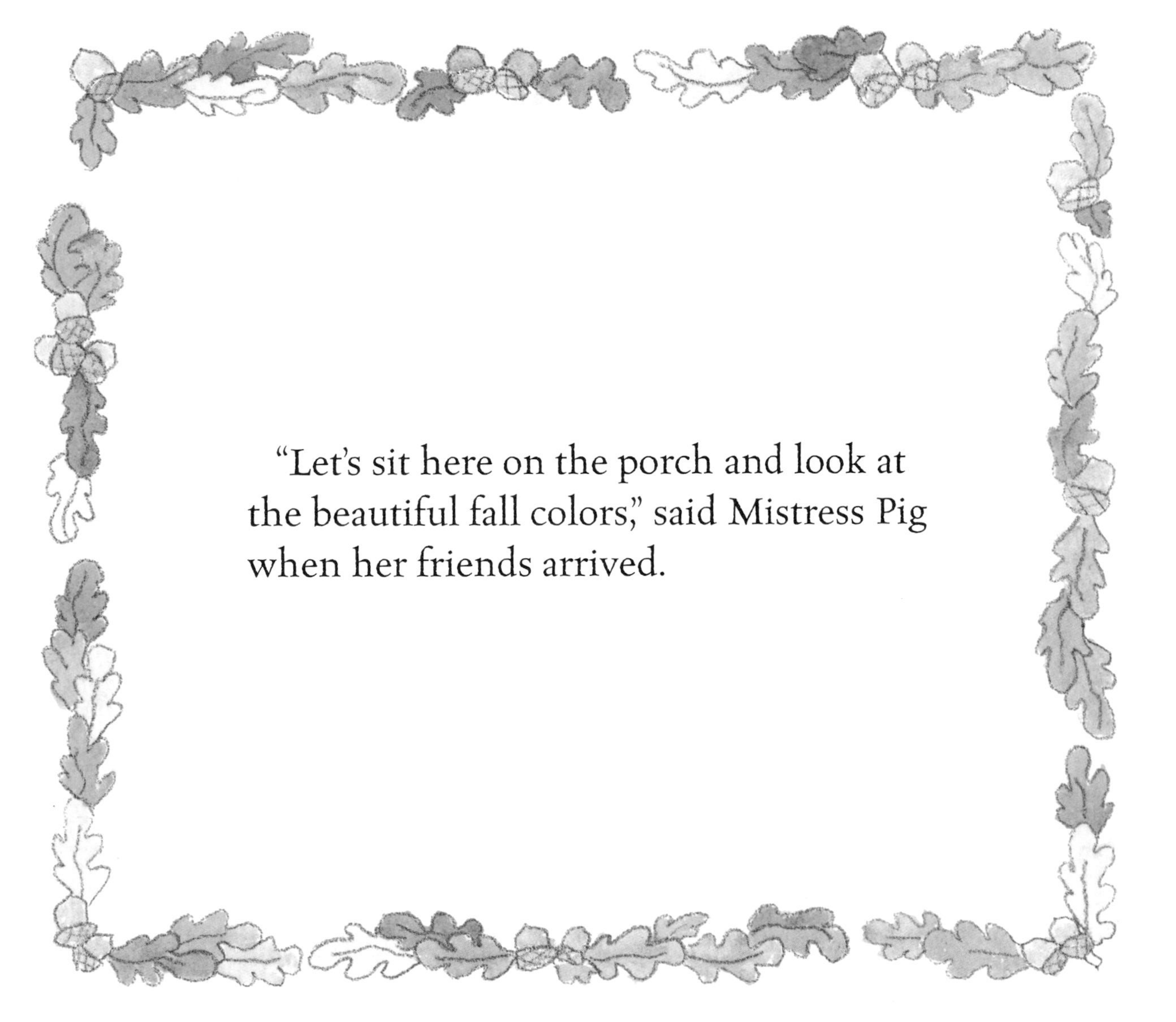

“Let’s sit here on the porch and look at the beautiful fall colors,” said Mistress Pig when her friends arrived.

"Won't you have a little punch?" she asked.

"You know, Piggy sweet, this is my favorite time of the year," said Missy Cat.

"Mine too, Kitty dear," said Mistress Pig. "That's why I wanted all of us to have a lovely dinner together."

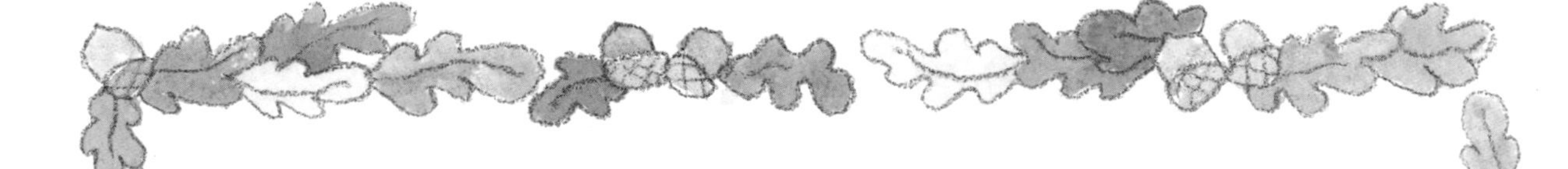

"Now, everyone sit down. I'm going out to the kitchen to put the finishing touches on the cucumber soup, the corn fritters, and the turnip soufflé."

The three friends sat.

They waited.

And waited.

And waited.

"I wonder what's keeping Piggy?" said Mister Frog.

"I'm hungry," growled Master Dog.

"Let's go see," said Missy Cat.

"Oh, Piggy!" said the three friends.

"I started tasting the soup, the fritters, the soufflé, and everything else to make sure they were all right—and I just couldn't stop," cried Mistress Pig. "Now I've ruined our dinner party."

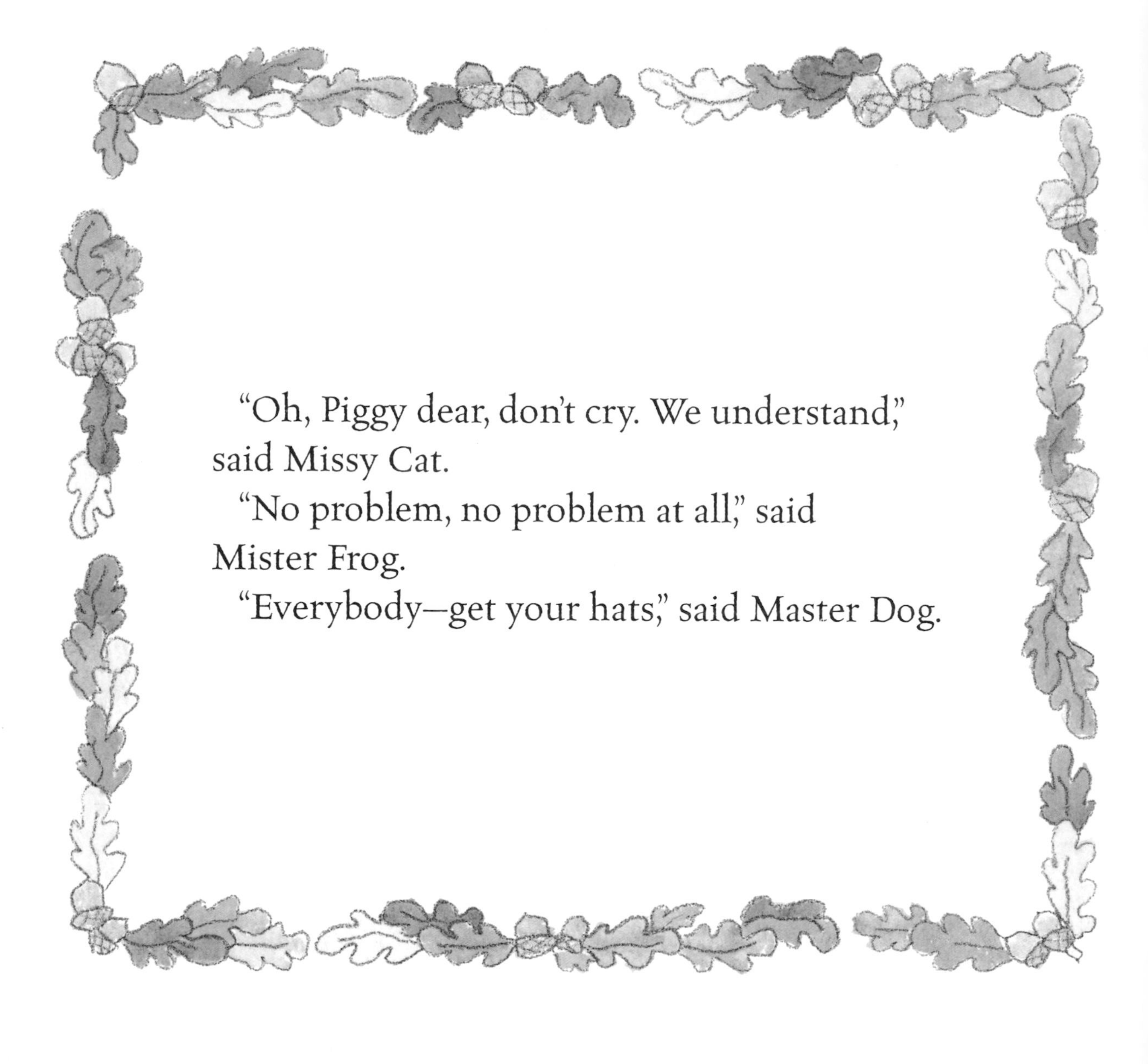

"Oh, Piggy dear, don't cry. We understand," said Missy Cat.

"No problem, no problem at all," said Mister Frog.

"Everybody—get your hats," said Master Dog.

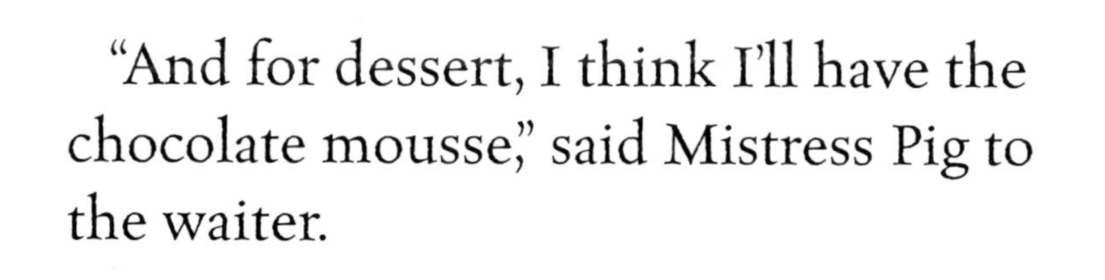

"And for dessert, I think I'll have the chocolate mousse," said Mistress Pig to the waiter.

"But Piggy, dessert comes *after* dinner!" said Mister Frog.